FR[illegible] ING
"RUBY'S STUDIO: THE FEELINGS SHOW"

Written by:
Samantha Kurtzman-Counter

Based on the screenplay by:
Ruby Vanderzee, Abbie Schiller & Samantha Kurtzman-Counter

Character design:
Valentina Ventimiglia
Book design:
Deborah Keaton

 Printed in Malaysia by Tien Wah Press — February 2013 — BkMiles20131— Library of Congress Control Number:2012949929 www.TheMotherCo.com

IT WAS AN EARLY SUNDAY MORNING,
AND LIKE EVERY OTHER SUNDAY MORNING,
MILES AND HIS LITTLE BROTHER MAX
PLAYED TOGETHER WHILE MOM MADE BREAKFAST.

MILES WAS A GREAT PUZZLE WIZARD.
MAX WAS A GREAT TRAIN CONDUCTOR.

GRRRR
AND ... LIKE EVERY OTHER SUNDAY MORNING,
MILES TRIED NOT TO MIND WHILE
LITTLE MAX PLAYED WITH ALL HIS TOYS.

MILES HAD **THE COOLEST TOYS.** ESPECIALLY THAT SUPER SHINY MODEL AIRPLANE DADDY AND MILES MADE TOGETHER.

UH... OH.
NOOO!!
DOOOON'T!

AND THAT IS WHEN

MILES GOT MAD.

HIS CHEEKS GOT **BURNING HOT**. HIS CHEST FELT TIGHT.

HIS HANDS **CURLED INTO FISTS**.

MY FAVORITE AIRPLANE! YOU BROKE IT! YOU ALWAYS BREAK **EVERYTHING!!**
SNIFF!
MAAAA MAAAAA!
LITTLE MAX RAN OUT OF MILES' ROOM.

MILES DIDN'T CARE. HE FELT **SO MAD** HE COULD **BURST!**
HE GRABBED HIS PLANE AND WAS ABOUT TO HURL IT ACROSS THE ROOM
WHEN SUDDENLY... HE CAUGHT A GLIMPSE OF HIMSELF IN THE MIRROR!

(GASP!) WHO ARE YOU?
INSTEAD OF SEEING HIS OWN REFLECTION,
HE SAW A FURRY RED MONSTER WITH HORNS,
LARGE ROUND EYES, AND FUNNY TEETH.

I'M **MAD**. I'M WHAT YOU FEEL LIKE INSIDE WHEN YOU'RE REALLY **MAD AND YELLING**.
THE FURRY MONSTER SAID.

GO AWAY!
YELLED MILES AT THE TOP OF HIS LUNGS.

I CAN'T, BECAUSE THE MORE YOU YELL, THE BIGGER, AND STRONGER, AND SCARIER I GET!

THEN I WILL BE MEAN AND I'LL HIT YOU!
SNAPPED MILES.
HITTING IS NOT OK! YOU MIGHT HURT YOURSELF OR SOMEONE ELSE. WOULD THAT MAKE YOU FEEL ANY BETTER?

I GUESS NOT, BUT
I DON'T KNOW WHAT TO DO.
I JUST FEEL
SO ... SO ... MAD!

WELL THEN LET'S FIGURE OUT WHAT YOU CAN DO TO FEEL BETTER. WHY DON'T YOU TRY HITTING THAT PILLOW?
MILES GAVE IT A TRY. HE HIT HIS PILLOW AS HARD AS HE COULD. BUT HE STILL FELT MAD.

HOW ABOUT TELLING ME WHAT'S MAKING YOU SO MAD?
I WANT MY AIRPLANE TO BE THE WAY IT WAS! I'M SO MAD MY LITTLE BROTHER BROKE IT.

AS MILES WAS TALKING, THE **MOST AMAZING THING** HAPPENED. THE MAD MONSTER STARTED TO SHRINK!

HE GOT SMALLER...

AND SMALLER...

AND SMALLER.

I JUST MADE THIS AIRPLANE AND IT'S SPECIAL TO ME. MAX IS **ALWAYS BREAKING THINGS.** HE'S TOO LITTLE TO KNOW HOW TO DO THINGS RIGHT.

USING YOUR WORDS IS REALLY HELPING! HOW DO YOU FEEL NOW?
(SIGH). ... WELL, I GUESS I'M A LITTLE SAD. I KINDA YELLED AT HIM AND NOW I FEEL BAD.

THE MAD MONSTER WAS NOW TEENY TINY. HE SMILED AND SAID,
BECAUSE YOU LEARNED HOW TO **CONTROL YOUR MAD FEELINGS**, I'M ALMOST ALL GONE.
MILES' CHEEKS WERE NO LONGER HOT. HIS CHEST WAS NO LONGER TIGHT. HIS HANDS WERE SOFT. NOW FULLY CALM, HE PICKED UP HIS BROKEN PLANE AND GENTLY TRIED TO PUT IT BACK TOGETHER.

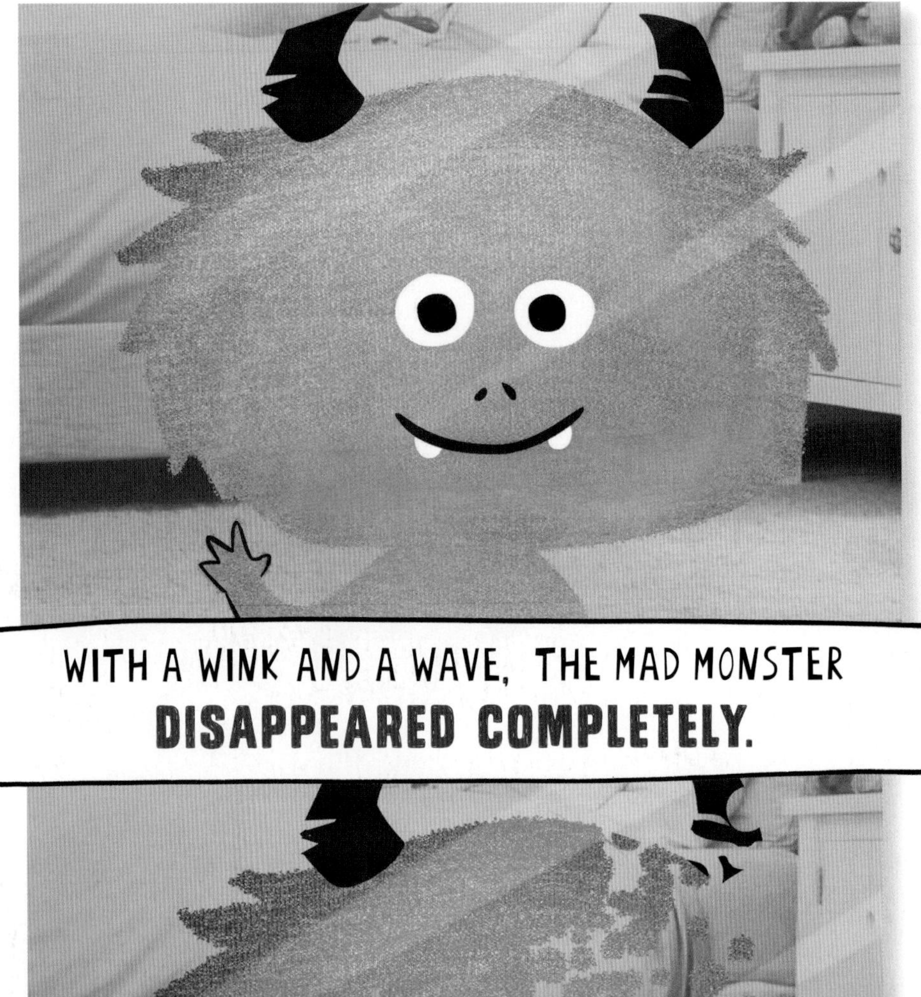

WITH A WINK AND A WAVE, THE MAD MONSTER
DISAPPEARED COMPLETELY.

WHEN MILES LOOKED BACK UP AT THE MIRROR, HE WAS SURPRISED TO SEE HIS VERY OWN REFLECTION. HE REALIZED HE DIDN'T FEEL MAD AT ALL ANYMORE.
WHAT'S GOING ON IN HERE?
JUST THEN, HIS MOTHER WALKED IN WITH SCARED LITTLE MAX.

MAX BROKE
MY PLANE, BUT
HE DIDN'T MEAN TO DO IT.
WANNA HELP ME TRY
TO FIX IT?
MILES GRABBED SOME GLUE.
MAX WAS SO HAPPY, HE RUSHED TO HIS BIG BROTHER'S SIDE.

AND BECAUSE MILES LEARNED TO **TALK THROUGH HIS MAD FEELINGS**
ON THIS EARLY SUNDAY MORNING, MILES AND HIS LITTLE BROTHER MAX
GOT TO **PLAY TOGETHER AGAIN** WHILE MOM MADE BREAKFAST.

A NOTE TO PARENTS AND TEACHERS

One of the biggest challenges for parents and educators of young children is finding a way to help young kids appropriately manage their anger. Tantrums and rage in children can be incredibly upsetting – and often scary – for both children and caregivers. The overwhelming nature of angry feelings makes them very hard to regulate, and children benefit by knowing concrete tools that can help.

In *When Miles Got Mad*, readers will learn alongside Miles that while anger sometimes feels like a big, scary monster inside you, "using your words" can lessen those overwhelming feelings and bring you to a better understanding of your anger – and yourself. By seeing Miles learn to manage his Mad Monster, young readers are empowered to understand, express, and move through their own anger.

It is our aim at The Mother Company to help parents, teachers and children with exactly these types of essential social and emotional challenges. *When Miles Got Mad* is the newest book in our award-winning Feelings Series, designed to enhance social and emotional literacy in young children. Research repeatedly shows that children who have the tools to navigate their challenging feelings have more success in school, work, and relationships throughout life; it is our goal to help along the way.

– Abbie Schiller & Sam Kurtzman-Counter, The Mother Company Mamas

Guided by the mission to "Help Parents Raise Good People," The Mother Company offers world-renowned expert advice for parents at TheMotherCo.com, as well as the "Ruby's Studio" line of award-winning products for children.

RUBY'S STUDIO is a line of HELPFUL, FUN, AWARD-WINNING PRODUCTS designed to enhance communication, cooperation, and self-understanding in young children.

Videos

Toys & Activities

Mobile Apps & eBooks

Enriching Books

What people are saying:

"We love Ruby's Studio!"
-Jennifer Garner, Actress & Mother

"A must in every young child's library"
-Betsy Brown Braun, Author and Parenting Expert

"Edutainment at its best"
-Daily Candy

Helping Parents Raise Good People:
RubysStudio.com